Animals' Guide to the Human Race
* Third Edition *

D.E. Kendall

Animals' Guide to the Human Race
D.E. Kendall

Dedicated to all the wonderful animals (*and humans!*) who inspire me…

Also, special dedication goes to my late grandmother, Elsie, who believed in me and always supported my writing.

Dear Human,

Thanks to top-secret, high-specification, super-technical apparatus (*and a thesaurus*), we've cast our thoughts unto paper for the *very first time*. While we understand this may come as a bit of a shock as we're so tolerant, there is a lot about humans that we find, well, *weird*.

Initially, we compiled this guide for fellow subservient species, with a view to helping them understand the strange ways of the imperious Homo Sapien. However, that top-secret, high-specification, super-technical apparatus we mentioned earlier was destroyed in an 'accident' (*likely by human overlords terrified of our 'inevitable rise to power'*).

Therefore, we've had no choice but to rely on our human friends to craft this introduction, to explain that we're now presenting *you* with this underrated masterpiece of science, so you can have a laugh on your lunch break, on holiday, or on the loo.

We hope our observations of your perplexing species are as amusing and confusing as you are to us. *Plus*, our bite-sized contributions are so short that they won't take up much of your unfathomably hectic schedule.

Sincerely,
Animals

Contents

Small Pets.................................. 1

#21 Syrian Hamster 2
#29 Guinea-Pig 7
#30 Lop Rabbit 8
#35 Budgerigar 11

Cats..................................... 13

#51 Bengal Cat 14
#52 British Shorthair 21
#53 Tabby Cat 24
#54 Ginger Cat 26
#55 Siamese Cat 30
#56 Calico Cat 33
#59 Ragdoll Cat 35

Dogs 38

#61 Dalmatian 39
#62 C.K.C. Spaniel 42
#64 Labrador 46
#67 Collie cross 50
#68 Great Dane 53
#70 Springer Spaniel 56
#72 Golden Retriever cross 57
#74 Jack Russell cross 58
#75 Yorkshire Terrier 62
#78 Staffordshire Bull Terrier 64

Horses **66**

#81 Welsh Section D 67
#82 Piebald Cob cross 68
#83 Dutch Warmblood cross 70
#86 Thoroughbred 73
#94 Anglo-Arabian Horse 77
#100 Connemara cross 82

Exotic Pets **84**

#101 Pygmy Hedgehog 85
#104 Cockatoo 86
#109 Bearded Dragon 87
#110 Chameleon 88

Farm Residents **89**

#40 Dexter Cow 90
#41 Holstein-Friesian 91
#44 Jacob Ram 92
#45 Cheviot Ewe 94
#46 Saddleback Sow 97

Zoo Residents **98**

#3 Chimpanzee 99
#4 Marmoset 101
#6 Elephant 102
#8 Rhinoceros 104
#13 Python 107
#15 Penguin 109

SMALL
PETS

Contributor #21
Syrian Hamster

Humans *know* they're incapable of maintaining their rule for much longer. I've studied them for most of my two years, so *I know* humans fear the artificial intelligence they've created, because they believe it'll eventually fight for control. However, human fear of AI is an effective cover, since it allows their least likely foe to effortlessly rise to power.

For around a century, we've snuggled our way into human affections – proving, once and for all, that world domination is our destiny.

While we were once mere meals for larger species, the hamster has risen to a position of great power in relatively little time. Humans, on the other paw, have supposedly taken tens of thousands of years to domesticate themselves; inadvertently opening the door for others to use their advancements to progress beyond the realms of humanity.

According to genetic history, as passed down from my mother, my ancestors once roamed miles at dusk in search of seeds and insects. Prior to our first positive encounters with humanity, hamsters were chased from burrows, trapped, and eaten. Life was tough. Therefore, the realisation that the human brain turns to mush upon experiencing our incredible cuteness was to become our greatest triumph.

While I'm still expected to eat seeds from time to time, I'm pleased that insects are no longer on the menu (*I tried a spider once; I do not recommend it*). Although they provide me with a varied diet, humans keep me trapped in a cage – when they're not shoving me into a plastic ball to watch me spin around the kitchen floor, that is. In fact, following one especially humiliating stint in the ball (*involving the dog, a chew toy, and a case of mistaken identity*), I managed to escape and immersed myself in the unlimited domain of the human.

It was upon that expedition around the house that I realised just how easily the human authority could be rattled.

First, I was forced to navigate the slippery kitchen floor while simultaneously dodging the dribbly dog, human hand scoops, and giant socked feet. Luckily, I made it to the carpeted hallway, where I scurried through the beige pasture and into the living room.

That living room was the chosen location for their various thrones. Along with their thrones, humans stored several significant technologies to display their ruling prowess, such as an enormous rectangular screen, a fiery hole in the wall surrounded by a shelf, and a mirror (*for them to watch behind their backs*).

I decided it was *my duty* to undermine human rule. Therefore, I squeezed my curvaceous frame behind the screen stand, discovered a colourful array of communication lines running into the screen, then chewed through those lines to sever human contact with their co-conspirators.

Next, fleeing the crime scene as swiftly as possible, I scuttled my way to the base of a huge stairway. The colossal collection of steps was stacked towards a skylight, where sunshine streamed through to warm yet more of that beige pasture humans love so much.

It seemed an insurmountable task, yet the sounds of frantic searching were heading in my direction, and I couldn't let the humans stuff me back into that ball. So, with all my might, I launched myself up the first step. If it weren't for my teeth, I'd have fallen at the first hurdle, yet somehow, I managed to clamber onto the step. I was in awe of my triumph. But there wasn't time to bask in my awesomeness, so I set to work tackling the next step.

About five steps up, I realised there was a hamster-sized ramp leading right to the top. Instead of dwelling on the fact I'd wasted a decent amount of micro-hibernation energy, I dashed my way up the ramp and found myself on yet another slippery surface.

There were giant, white, shiny surfaces towering above me. I sensed an uncomfortable dampness, which I found incredibly unsettling. Strong chemical scents grabbed at my nose, by which time I heard human footsteps thundering up the stairway. At that point, I had no other choice than to shimmy up the nearest surface before slipping into the freezing void of a sink – not unlike the kitchen sink, except it didn't contain soiled human eating utensils.

I grappled with the slippery surface of the sink in my attempt to escape, though tumbled back down into a cumbersome heap time and again. As humans noisily clambered through the entrance, I accepted my fate as I sulked, trapped beside the plughole.

Thankfully, however, an idea struck me as one of the humans scooped me into their cupped, sweaty palms: *weaponised teeth*.

No sooner had my teeth punctured their peachy flesh did the human shriek and drop me to the floor. I was thankful for the bedding I'd stored in my pouches, as it helped me bounce straight out of the damp room and back onto the beige pasture of the upper hallway.

Without a second's consideration, I bounded toward the nearest opening and found myself in one of their sleeping dens. The human nest was a mess of layered materials; the intense colours of which offended my eyes.

After the human had dropped me, I felt an act of resistance was appropriate, so I determined that interfering with their hibernation station would be a fitting act. I reached up for the materials dangling over the solid section of the nest and started climbing.

Upon reaching the top, the treasure I found was of immeasurable brilliance. It was the biggest, fluffiest, most inviting heap of materials I had *ever* seen.

The unmistakable sounds of disgruntled humans approached, snapping me from my reverie. I rushed over to the heap of materials and tore them open, diving in to the glorious nest of fluff. Before the humans entered the room, I'd shoved as much fluff as possible into the little space I had left in my pouches. Then, moments before a behemoth hand wrapped around my middle, I flicked clouds of fuzz from their nest – which angered the humans.

From my cage, I observe them.

My intention is to escape the confines within which they trap me without alerting them to my presence.

Then, I *will* find the route to world domination. It'll be *humans who live in cages*, and *I'll* be amused by watching them bash into the washing machine in translucent plastic balls.

Contributor #29
Guinea Pig

My humans regularly attempt to communicate with me, usually through a series of weird, squeaky sounds. Often, humans' squeaky sounds are accompanied by jangling toys or celery sticks. Sometimes, I wonder what life would be like if my humans could understand me…

If they could speak 'pig', humans could enjoy my extensive knowledge of vegetables, I'd be able to tell humans that my little accidents are a result of their squeezing my middle, and it'd be far easier to demand food whenever I'm hungry (*or bored*).

Since humans cannot understand our language, I feel it's my duty to teach them:
Growling and teeth chattering – warning that we're angry or in pain, so humans should ensure we're not injured or ill, then leave us alone.
Wheeking – these loud, high-pitched sounds indicate that we're excited, especially around feeding time or when we hear dinner being prepared. If we love our humans a lot, we'll 'wheek' at them for attention.
Bubbling and chutting – bubbly, purring sounds tell humans we are happy and content; especially when we're being cuddled gently, or we're fed our favourite treat!

Contributor #30
Lop Rabbit

It was a Thursday afternoon. The store had been quiet, much like any other Thursday afternoon. At some point, rain broke through a crash of thunder and pelted the steel roof overhead – as if an omen for the horror about to unfold.

Others chose to hide away from the unnerving sense of impending doom, but I did not. I sat in the open to await my fate.

Suddenly, at the very moment a bolt of lightning illuminated the dull car park, a fluffle of humans scrambled through the automatic doors and stumbled onto the shop floor. There were four of them – one adult, three kittens. *That poor adult didn't stand a chance.*

One of our carers greeted them with unease, and the smallest pointed a grubby finger straight at me. While the adult appeared to be encouraging their litter to ponder a hamster, it seemed my glossy coat was far too enticing, and the young ones made a dash for my enclosure. *The others were right to hide.*

All three of them smushed their soiled faces against the glass separating me from their germ-riddled aura. I refused to run away. I'd dealt with young humans before, I could do it again. This was what I'd been trained to do.

So, the carer carefully lifted me from the safety of my enclosure and placed me onto the lap of one of those humans. The stickiness of their hands grated against my aversion to grime, but, being the professional I was, I endured. That was, until the carer turned and the smallest human gripped my ears like the last slice of carrot from a food dish!

Instinctively, I span around and sunk my teeth into the sticky flesh of the littlest one. Upon retraction of my teeth, blood spurted from the holes I'd pierced in their hand like water from the fountain at the front of the store. The sound that leaked from the smallest human was almost as unbearable as it was satisfying, and I was flung to the cold concrete.

I hopped to my enclosure in hope I'd be returned home, but I wasn't. Instead, the adult human seemed so delighted by the situation that the carer scooped me into their arms and plonked me into a plastic carrier box with bars across its only entrance and exit.

The journey to hell was long but silent, aside the occasional spurt of sobbing from the smallest human.

Upon arrival, I was left to await my fate from a vantage point atop a shiny counter. As soon as my cell had been prepared, the adult released me into it.

There was barely the room to stretch. While I had free access to food, water, and a litter tray, I was located in the midst of human activity and forced to endure the booming sounds of a talking mirror, the constant patter of foul-smelling human feet, and relentless attempts by the adult to encourage me to eat carrot – as if they intended to taunt me.

It has been seven *long* years.

My punishment for damaging a human has cost me a life of luxury. Initially, I was employed by the adult to administer behavioural management; I was deployed whenever the young humans became unruly, because they were so terrified of me that my presence could instantly render them still and quiet.

However, I'm proud to say that my rehabilitation is going well, and I haven't tasted human flesh in over *three years*. I should be heading back to the store any day now!

Humans might be powerful, filthy creatures who know next to nothing about coat hygiene, but they certainly know their way around justice.

Contributor #35
Budgerigar

Humans can be so cruel. They force me to endure a boring diet of seeds and fruit, while I'm forced to watch them guzzle down the most delicious-looking meals, like pizza and spaghetti, as well as sweet treats, like cakes and ice cream. But, the most glorious food of all that I long to enjoy is the *biscuit*.

I ate a biscuit once. It was amazing. And it is beyond unfair that humans won't share with me. So, I plotted my revenge.

Having lived around humans for ten years, I've learned to understand their language. A phrase I'd heard crop up from time to time was, 'revenge is a dish best served cold'. While that was the basis of my original revenge plan, it soon became apparent that it wasn't true. I've watched many-a-biscuit plop into my humans' hot beverages, and the instant, fleeting sense of devastation it would cause gave me a wonderful idea – that revenge was not a dish at all, nor was it to be served cold.

I employed my plan one gloriously sunny morning. When the humans released me from my cage for a wing-stretch, I scoped the living room and locked onto my target. I'd chosen to target a morning cup of coffee, the most sacred of hot beverages for humans.

Awaiting the perfect moment, and with ultimate precision, my revenge plopped straight into the mug with a satisfying splash.

Perching myself on the arm of a chair, I had an excellent vantage point from which to watch my revenge unravel. However, all the human did was sip their coffee, complain about the taste of 'the new milk', then continue to drink it as if there was nothing wrong!

The disappointment was intolerable. And, to add insult to injury, the human opened the special tin and munched through *five* biscuits right in front of me.

It wasn't until they reached the end of their drink that the human realised what I'd done. Just as I reached the safety of my cage, the human squealed in horror as they discovered my revenge on the bottom of their empty mug. No amount of tongue wiping or water seemed enough to dispel their discomfort.

That sense of satisfaction was *almost* as great as the forbidden taste of a biscuit.

CATS

Contributor #51
Bengal Cat

They adored me. A king among the elite and unworthy alike, I was the world's greatest show cat for two long, gloriously exciting, soul electrifying, scandalous weeks. Males wished they were in my paws; females wished they were in my travel crate. It was the craziest, most glamourous time of my life.

Alas, the lifestyle of celebrity is ultimately unsustainable. After an incident of miscommunication with a rather handsy judge – *that resulted in a tetanus jab* – I suffered a wave of bad press, which, subsequently, put an end to my glittering career in show-business.

I could've wasted my days dozing on windowsills, being hand-fed tuna until I was too fat to fit in my litter box, but I didn't. This is the story of how I transformed my life of luxury and glitz into a life of meaning and purpose. I selflessly ventured into the perilous realms of the human training profession.

Although a thankless task, I rose to the challenge of addressing the shortage of human staff who are of a decent calibre. Any cat can find a human, or several, willing to feed them, but the truly great humans, those dedicated to feline fidelity, are near impossible to find.

My own, impeccably behaved, human staff are the result of almost a decade of hardcore training regimes. It took about four years to get them in line, but once I succeeded, boy, did they make my life worth living. Right now, there's a heated debate as to which human gets to take me to the vet for my yearly vaccination. However, this story is not about my human staff. This story is about the first human group I encountered when my own staff sent me on a retreat, to recuperate somewhere miles out of the spotlight after 'the incident'.

It was a crisp, autumnal morning. My staff courageously concealed their sorrow with smiling, as they handed my travel crate to the retreat's proprietor. As I was chauffeured towards the kitchen, the waft of hypervigilance breezed through my travel crate that I translated as 'feral cats not welcome'. There was a comforting lack of non-human scent in the building, just how I liked it.

They released me onto the pristine marble floor space, where I slid towards a human-grade water dish presented on a mat decorated with a fish motif. While I recognised their attempt at humour, I didn't appreciate it. Then, the human staff broke rank to greet me directly in turn. There were three of them: one female adult, one male adult, and one offspring.

While the female's scent was ineffectually mild, the male reeked heavily of spice, and the offspring leaked body odour to offensive intensity. I swiftly detected a struggle for superiority, since the adults' acceptance of the stench of the offspring was indication of their submission to him. My initial observation anticipated challenge.

I realised from the outset that this was no retreat, it was my *calling*.

After allowing the humans a couple of hours to adjust to my presence – by rubbing against every surface with a corner, to spread my scent subtly – I made the decision to target adult female first.

She was enthusiastic about my presence, which was a positive start. I appreciated her efforts to hand-feed me pieces of chicken, until I realised she was offering chicken thigh meat instead of chicken breast. Apparently, staring at the pieces of meat she dropped onto the kitchen floor in front of me wasn't enough of a signal for her to stop. So, I walked away.

In walking away from the human, she quickly learned that her behaviour was unacceptable, and she cleared up the chicken before following me into the lounge. There was a sumptuous, crushed velvet, three-piece suite set equidistant to a huge, rectangle viewing window atop an ornate fireplace.

The lighting was ambient, and curtains were drawn, so when the human illuminated the viewing window with the magic doofer, I knew what was about to happen.

As she settled into the sanctuary of the sofa, directly across from the viewing window, she scooped me from the white carpet and plonked me onto her lap. The gentle, repetitive stroking motion was relaxing, at first. I let out an inadvertent purr at one point, which delighted the human. However, as the music reverberating about the room became tense, so did the human. Those once delicate smoothing motions began to speed up with the tempo of the music, and the inane chatter she'd been showering me with ceased. Eventually, I feared for my glossy coat, as I felt the tension of the viewing window seep through the human's nails and into my back. *Enough was enough.*

I released my claws from their dormant station and dug them right in to the human's legs. She leapt from that sofa with such speed that I was flung from her lap!

Flicking my tail in derision, I strode from the lounge, expecting her to follow. She did follow, and even proceeded to give me a bowl full of extravagant salmon treats that my usual human staff saved for vet visits and sock exchanges. From that moment on, the adult female's guilt kept her securely in my debt.

The adult male was a different kettle of fish. Contrary to the female, adult male human was disinterested in my presence. *Unacceptable.*

At that juncture in my human training journey, I determined that some conflicts required tact, whereas others demanded brute force. In the instance of my second human training subject, the latter was chosen.

Intimidation is easier if the subject acknowledges your existence. No amount of hissing, threatening stares, or angry tail flicks were enough to rouse a reaction from the adult male. There was a point at which I followed him into the toileting room and watched him urinate, yet he *still* didn't respond to my company.

In that agonising hour I spent following the adult male, I had determined something important. I noted that he adored the white carpet of the lounge, stairway, upper hallway, and sleeping quarters far more deeply than he considered his fellow humans. If another human so much as gestured at placing the toe of a shoe onto that carpet, adult male flew into a frenzied rage. Others may have mistaken his volume for authority, though I did not. I perceived adult male's adoration of the carpet as a weakness prime for exploitation.

So, as mealtimes were rarely held in the lounge, the humans' decision to eat pizza in front of the viewing window one evening played right into my paws. As they were settling down with their boxes of oily, flat, tomato mush bread – following a lengthy lecture about the carpet – I stealthily hopped onto the arm of the chair upon which the carpet professor was sat. It was the audacity of the human to shoo me from the arm of the chair that sparked my plan into action, as I pounced onto his pizza box and dragged it to the carpet with me.

The upturned box was enough to draw a tear from his eye, as the adult male melodramatically lifted the cardboard box to reveal his upside-down circular bread. As he slowly peeled the pizza from its resting place, he revealed a tomato mush spatter pattern embedded into the once immaculate white carpet. I vacated the room as voices reached fever pitch, seconds before there was a mad dash to the kitchen for detergent and towels.

He may not have liked me, though the adult male did respect me from that moment on; he never shooed me again.

Moving on to the offspring, I sensed resistance afoot. While we shared a few similarities – neither of us went outside by choice, for example – I was painfully aware that I'd taken on a mammoth challenge.

Seemingly uninterested in other life forms, the insufferable creature spent much of his time staring into the abyss of a handheld device. I was unfamiliar with the young of the species, so initially I approached the offspring with great caution.

Usually found huddled in a corner, light from the device illuminating his pimply face full of angst, I had no way of snapping the offspring's attention onto me without resorting to the use of my claws. While I advocate the use of claws, teeth, and a well-aimed tail flick during a human training programme, I draw the line at using negative reinforcement on human young. Instead, as I discovered with the offspring in this particular training endeavour, irritation works wonders.

There was, on occasion, an instance when the human offspring would relieve themselves of the handheld device in favour of a larger device attached to a hard, knobbly mat that made 'tapping' sounds. I did not appreciate those incessant tapping sounds when I was trying to take a nap after a busy morning spent sharpening my claws behind the curtains.

So, I leapt up onto the tabletop, and I settled myself onto the hands of the offspring, upon the knobbly mat. Simultaneously confused and terrified by my actions, the offspring's hands trembled beneath my beautiful body as they stared wide-eyed at my shapely frame. Moments later, the offspring cried out for his mother, who rushed in, paused, then laughed.

Contributor #52
British Shorthair Cat

The subject of my advice about humanity rests on the issue of dealing with human spawn. They're unhygienic, they're unpleasant, and they are, quite frankly, unhelpful.

Once – *on one of those endless summer days when all three human spawn have nowhere else to be* – I gestured for the youngest to reach some catnip for me. Female servant, mother of spawn, had hidden my catnip from the dog, but she wasn't around to retrieve it for me. There was *no way* I was risking my fourteenth life to climb onto the fridge, so, the smallest human spawn was my only option.

Unfortunately, the spawn mistook my gesture for affection, and scooped me into her sticky arms before I could escape.

Bright pink walls burned my corneas, as the spawn jolted me about in her death grip, across the fluffy purple carpet of her lair. Without the energy to refuse, I was forced to endure half an hour (HALF AN HOUR) of tea party shenanigans, until I could escape when she left the room to refill a tiny teapot with toilet water. I avoid that spawn wherever possible, including any and all eye contact.

Male servant has few possessions, or family members, he cares for more deeply than a ball covered in scribbles that he keeps on the mantlepiece in the living room. There was an occasion that the eldest spawn was wreaking havoc with his noisy clowder, when they collectively decided to take the scribble ball down to play with it. Normally, I'd avoid rowdy spawn, but instinct suggested this was about to be quite the spectacle.

So, I watched the human spawn kick the ball about as they screeched with glee at their collective misbehaviour. Then, one of them lobbed the ball straight at me! Luckily, I have plenty of body padding, so the ball bounced off of me and landed in the centre of the room, rolling to a halt at the feet of the eldest.

All three of them watched on with horror as I jumped off the armchair, strode over to the ball, held out a paw, released my claws, then punctured the ball. As life squealed from the ball, like air from a balloon, colour drained from the faces of the spawn. I exited the room, passing male servant in the doorway; I heard his snivelling from the kitchen.

There are also three occasions a year that each of the human spawn has a celebration focused on them. Those 'parties' usually result in an exponential spike in female servant's stress levels. So, I take it upon myself to assist her.

Of course, I am not obliged to help, though I care about my staff (*and one can't beat a tuna sandwich swiped from the table when humans aren't looking*).

At 'parties' I preside over the food table. If any of the spawn, mine or not, attempt to take too much food, I growl at them like a panther until they back off. Obviously, human spawn are born with arrogance, so when one of them ignores my warning, I won't hesitate to stalk them until either they drop food for me, or I scram their ankles.

Contributor #53
Tabby Cat

Boxes are *the best* human invention in the whole, entire universe. Something *always* appears out of them – it's magic!

My humans hate that I love boxes. And they hate that I enjoy checking *every* box that passes through the front door. Sometimes, I like to sleep in boxes, which seems to irritate my humans, though I think they're just jealous, because they're *far* too big to sleep in boxes.

Some boxes are small, and I can't fit in them very comfortably, though I still try. The trick with small boxes is to wedge your legs in before your tummy. Once, I was especially proud of myself for squeezing in to a tiny box, when I got stuck because my tummy rolls trapped my legs inside. It took a whole *hour* for my humans to notice and rescue me!

Then, there's the thin boxes – they're the trickiest. As a kitten, I could slither right through skinny boxes. Now, I have to take a run-up across the kitchen floor and slide myself towards the box at speed, if there's any hope of making it through. Sometimes I succeed, so my humans clap and cheer, though other times I miss, and end up sliding straight into the kitchen counter.

Thick boxes are great to chew, until you have to go to the vet because you haven't pooped in three days. So, the trick is *not* to eat the cardboard as you chew it.

Some boxes are filled with strange, super-light blobs that you can swim in without water! I *love* to dive in to those boxes and send super-light blobs flying everywhere.

I enjoy tall boxes, too. They're the best to hide in and pop out to scare humans. I find it especially funny when a human is carrying a drink or some food; it goes *everywhere* when I jump out of a box at them!

Big, low-level boxes are my absolute favourite, however. In fact, I love them *so much* that my humans gave away the bed I wasn't using and put blankets in a box instead. To begin, I rub my scent *all over* the box and roll around in it, to soften the cardboard. Then, I'll scratch my claws around a little, to fluff up the bottom of the box and make some fun sounds that drive my humans mad.

Contributor #54
Ginger Cat

I am unhappy with the human attitude toward food. Humans don't respect the good, old-fashioned tradition of working for one's meal. Satisfied with ready-packaged edibles, humans go about their wasteful feeding habits without appreciation or a sense of achievement.

Despite my best efforts, spending all night every night hunting for a special meal to gift those ingrates, I am yet to receive thanks. I provide a catch so fresh that sometimes it isn't even dead (*to encourage some much-needed mental stimulation*), though all I receive in return is a stern scolding and banishment from the house for a few hours. Disgraceful.

My usual targets tend to be rats, mice, voles, sponges, frogs, toads, rogue socks, birds, and fish from the pond next door. I keep my mind and body active by pursuing some of nature's most weird and wonderful creatures.

Though I'll be honest, I'm worried about my humans. They spend *so much time* staring at flashy screens and ignoring each other that I don't think it'll be long before they lose the ability to communicate naturally. They don't even use the dining table anymore, just eat meals from trays balanced on their laps.

So, I took responsibility into my own paws; I wasn't going to let their brains turn to mush without a fight!

I selected a mouse to execute my plan, since mice scare the living daylights out of humans. Plus, they scuttle about more quickly than fish, who just boringly flop about when given a chance to escape my wrath.

It was important to time my plan to perfection, because it was rare that all humans were awake simultaneously.

I selected a crisp, spring, Sunday morning. The humans had attended an event together the previous night called a 'wedding' and mentioned how they regretted 'all the prosecco'. Both adults and adolescents were in a similar state of lethargy when they emerged, which was ideal for my master plan.

Careful to catch it by its tail, I carried the squirming mouse through my personal entrance in the garden door, straight into the living room. The humans were slouched in silence, two on the sofa, two on chairs, and the adults sipped coffee while the adolescents dozed with arms over their faces. Nobody noticed me walk into the room, I may as well have been invisible.

Then, as planned, I released the wriggling vermin. It dropped to the floor with a surprising thud, considering how small it was, and proceeded to dart about the carpet in a mad panic. Initially, there was screaming. The adults were the first to jump onto the furniture, while one adolescent started filming the mouse on their smart telephone and the other watched in stunned silence as if they were dreaming.

What didn't go to plan, however, was that the mouse sensed the humans' fear and stopped darting about frantically. Realising it could make creatures five-hundred times bigger than it dance around in terror, it began intimidating them by threatening to jump onto the furniture, too!

I leapt onto the arm of a chair, where I could watch calamity unfold from a better vantage point. Though I needn't have bothered, since the mouse suddenly changed its strategy and raced out of the living room towards the kitchen. We all followed, in amazement.

The mouse managed to clamber up onto the bin, hop onto a counter, then parkour across the sink full of dirty dishes, before reaching a flowerpot on the windowsill for a breather.

A plan was rapidly forged between the four humans as the mouse was resting in the flowerpot. They intended to place an upside-down saucepan over it, flip it, slam a lid onto the saucepan, and release the cocky little creature outside – presumably so I could catch it again.

Unfortunately for them, the mouse could understand them far better than I could.

The saucepan was inches from the mouse when it launched itself into the air towards the human approaching it, before landing on the slippery kitchen floor and – I kid you not – it slid the length of the kitchen like an ice dancer, before escaping through my personal entrance in the garden door.

Subsequently, I was banned from the house until dusk. The humans were not impressed by my efforts to engage them in some harmless hunting, so, I'll steer clear of using mice in the future. I'm thinking frogs might be the answer…

Contributor #55
Siamese Cat

The *canine* – humanity's answer to their superiority complex.

Dogs help humans feel a sense of superiority, thanks to their weakness for attention. However, humans inherently understand that felines are above them in nature's hierarchy, which is the reason I am able to state, confidently, the truth of it all.

There are the standard superiority behaviours (*not allowing dogs onto kitchen counters, disallowing the dismantle of furnishing fabrics, forcing them to perform tricks for treats, etc.*) then there are the fundamental superiority behaviours that separate canines from felines in the eyes of humanity, which I shall explore in greater detail here…

Toileting, or, 'doing business' if you prefer, is part and parcel of existence. Therefore, it is a basic right that every creature has a safe, sanitary location in which to carry out their deposits. Owing to my role as leader of the household, I am provided with my own toileting tray in three separate locations – I may make transactions in peace and privacy, without worry over poor weather or unsavoury scents, since my humans enjoy cleaning my environment for me.

In contrast, they expect the dog to leave the premises to complete their dealings outside, in all weathers. I tested the theory that humans perceive the dog as their inferior, by gently encouraging the dog to unload their assets in the bath. After all, when I paid the bath a visit for that same purpose, the humans reacted with great humour and seemed only mildly offended. But, when the dog paid the bath a visit, the humans reacted most dramatically; the level of disgust displayed by the humans was unprecedented! Not only did they scold the dog verbally about what he'd done, but they banned him from the bathroom for it.

Another major difference that separates me from the dog is the human reaction to gifts. To thank them for their service, I provide gifts for the humans on a regular basis. Although there are times when the humans react unfavourably to my offerings, in general, my gifts are met with gratitude and a flurry of activity as the humans rush to prepare my gifts for their bin sacrifice or the garden ritual – whereby a lifeless gift gets dropped into the receptacle and presented to the coveted 'bin men' (*for whom my humans scramble to make offerings in time each week*), or, their squirming gift gets taken to the garden in a dash of terror (*presumably to return it to Mother Nature lest it raid the pantry, again*). When the dog presented the humans with a snail last week, plopping it directly onto their lap as they ate pizza in the lounge, there was screaming and smashed plates as they scrambled to avoid the ornate gastropod. And, when he tried to hand one of them a ball yesterday, the trail of slobber that followed its path as it rolled across the dinner table seemed to displease the humans greatly. Apparently, they do not accept tokens of gratitude from the dog as readily as they accept gifts from me.

And, finally, there's the issue of comfort. I may make myself comfortable upon the lap of whichever human I wish – they are so afraid to upset me that they remain very still beneath my voluptuous frame. However, should the dog decide to ascend the sofa to place himself upon the lap of a human, the reaction is far less favourable. The dog's ungainly clambering is often met with groans of pain and an eventual shove from the humans – I assume that's largely to do with the dog's rancid breath; and the fact he's a Great Dane who thinks he's a cat.

Contributor #56
Calico Cat

I adore the festive season! The twinkly lights, the food, and, *best of all*, the tree my humans drag indoors to decorate with gifts for me.

My humans are so thoughtful, bringing me a tree when it's cold outside so I can practise my hunting skills indoors.

I'm assuming the reason they hang dead sparkly gifts on the tree is because I collect *so many* gifts for them throughout the year that it's their way of thanking me.

If I had to choose my favourite thing about the tree, it *has to be* the shimmering string they call 'tinsel'. I guess humans put tinsel on the tree to give me more of a challenge, since the year there was no tinsel, I removed *every* gift from the tree in the time it took my humans to return from that place they love to go called 'food shopping'. Ever since, they've remembered to put tinsel on the tree, and every year, *without fail*, I get tangled in it and have to dangle from the branches until one of my humans comes to the rescue.

Throughout the festive season just gone, I spent hours sneaking gifts from the tree when my humans weren't looking (*same as when I hunt live gifts outside, my humans don't like*

*watching when I hunt because it makes them
jealous and annoyed*) and hiding the gifts in new
places for them to find. So far, they've been
pretty rubbish at finding my gifts – for instance,
just the other day we had something called a
'guest' in the empty sleeping room where I hid a
few gifts; that guest was *not* happy to find a
pointy, highly breakable, glittery gift under their
pillow. We haven't seen that guest since.

Something else I like to do for my
humans when it's icy outside – to show how
grateful I am that they go to all that trouble to
put a tree indoors for me – is to warm their
shoes. I've noticed that humans tend to
complain a lot about freezing in the wintertime,
and I wouldn't want my humans to freeze; *who
would feed me?* So, whenever I notice their
shoes are cold, I pee in them.

Although the human reaction to soggy
shoes is often shock and disgust to begin with, I
always note that hint of gratitude as they realise
how well it warms their frozen toes. I would sit
on their shoes, but I don't like to waste precious
time that could be spent playing in my special
gift tree.

Contributor #59
Ragdoll Cat

The greatest oddity of the human race is their fascination with bathing. I cannot, for the life of me, fathom the reason humans relish stewing in their own filth like soup in a pot.

Water is meant for drinking, *not* for washing oneself. Their futile attempts to bathe me in the sink (*of all places*) ended with a slippery kitchen floor, a foot injury, and fifteen stitches (*for the humans, not for me*). After that incident, I steer clear if water is in the vicinity, if at all possible.

I took it upon myself, many moons ago, to convey to my ignorant clowder of humans that there's a higher purpose for their tongue beyond mere food consumption. As a purist, I am adept at grooming myself to perfection with only my tongue. It was my sincerest hope that humans would learn from my lessons in appropriate cleaning methods, though as of yet, my attempts have proven fruitless…

My first port of call was to lead by example. Therefore, whenever my humans were gathered in the living room to melt their minds watching television, I would position myself centrally on the wooden platform – in front of said television – and lick every inch of my body.

Initially, my lecture on life skills would be met with hostility, as they'd try to slide me off the platform with a cushion. However, my resolve far outweighs theirs, and I continued to repeat the lesson every evening for months, until I realised the message was not getting through.

The second lesson in my bathing course involved a physical element, namely, discomfort. Humans learn far more quickly if they can associate a lesson with a lack of comfort – for instance, should a human burn their hand on the stove, they aren't going to repeat that behaviour because it caused them discomfort. So, using my new perspective, I completed a little research and observed that humans are very private creatures when it comes to bathing. That was the inspiration for slipping into the bathroom – through the bathroom window, which is always jammed open, or through the bathroom door, if left ajar – and positioning myself atop the human deposit station. From such a strategic vantage point, I could stare directly into my human's eyes as they'd float unhygienically in their own watery filth. Usually, the human would take to complaint or bribery in hope of sending me away, though when that was unsuccessful, they would resort to flinging items at me, *soap dispensers and the like*, until I retired from the lesson. In fear of my own safety, that form of teaching lasted a few short lessons. Humans would prefer to remain concealed within the putrid vat of bubbles – until their skin resembles a dried-up prune – than to get out and reveal their embarrassingly fluff-less form as they chastise me.

Finally, I was left with no choice but to resort to an extreme method of teaching that involves a component of disgust. While I am not proud of the lesson I am about to disclose, I would like to convey its importance in achieving the desired result. As the remaining option in my arsenal, I took to 'mistaking' the bath for a litter tray. The act of elimination in that pointless tub of suds, unseen, *moments before a human entered it*, had them splashing about and scrambling to get out, causing them to face plant the floor in a most ungainly fashion as they cussed and hissed at me to leave. I am thankful to announce that my human clowder has not since braved a bath.

DOGS

Contributor #61
Dalmatian

I *love* humans. The main reasons I love humans are the food, the fusses, and the walkies, but, I also love that they bring some awesome robots into our house. Unfortunately, some robots behave differently for me compared to how they behave for humans…

Washing Machine is this magical robot who swallows dirty materials, swirls them around in its tummy, squirts bubbly digestive juices all over them, spins them really fast before beeping to let my humans know their materials are clean. It's an amazingly clever creature, but it *always* makes me dizzy. No matter how long I sit beside it, Washing Machine refuses to answer to my commands regarding chicken and biscuits, and instead, chooses to spin for my humans. I will keep trying to befriend the mystical robot, in hope that one day it will accept my commands too.

Television is *amazing*. Not only does Television hypnotise my humans, sometimes for hours on end, it's also able to make them laugh, cry, or fall asleep. I'm able to do most of those things for humans too, but always when I'm not intending for them to laugh or cry (*like that time*

I was so excited about the new sofa that I bounced up and down on it to look out of the window, straight after running in from the garden because it was raining, which made the younger humans laugh and the older humans cry). However, the most impressive trick that Television can perform is to make other dogs appear in the living room, then make them vanish as if they weren't there! I can't help but shout praise at Television when it does that, despite the fact it seems to irritate my humans, who prefer not to praise the robots who work for them.

Toilet, however, is the most dangerous but exciting of the house robots. While my humans prefer to use the automatic drinking portal in privacy, I'm just grateful that Toilet does what I want – unlike most of the other house robots. Humans can be uber-protective of Toilet, though since I've learned how to open the door to its nesting place, I'm able to access it when they aren't home. So, Toilet has this special lid that acts as a filtration system *and* as a water protector, which means the water within it has a slightly different taste to dull normal water, and the water within it doesn't contain hair or bits of human dust like my boring water bowl does. But, it's important to lift *both* parts of the special lid up when using the drinking portal, because I made the mistake of lifting just

the top layer, and ended up wearing the special
lid! I had that thing dangling around my neck for
what seemed like ages as I waited for my
humans to get home. I couldn't fit around the
corner at the top of Stairs with the special lid
swinging from my neck either, so I had to sit
there and wait for them. *Three* of my humans
had to work together to wiggle the special lid off
my head.

Oven is my most favourite robot of all.
Toilet may be talented at summoning fresh
water, but Oven is an expert at creating *the best*
smells. Humans are even more protective of
Oven than they are of any other robot in the
house. I often spend my evenings staring into
the glowing heart of Oven, as it transforms
containers of slop into magnificent meals. It's
impossible not to drool while staring into the
wonder of Oven's magic at work, though that's
a small price to pay for the incredible edibles it
creates. Humans try to keep Oven's magic to
themselves, but eventually, I *always* manage to
persuade them to share their bounty with me
(*thanks to my superpower – 'the stare'*).

Contributor #62
Cavalier King Charles Spaniel

I've had the same humans my entire life, so I cannot speak for other humans, though mine have a selfish streak in matters involving cake.

While my humans are usually prepared to toss me the occasional scrap of chicken or the odd crumb of piecrust, they are *never* willing to share their greatest human delicacy – the cake.

After *years* of being denied access to the wonder that is cake, of being forced to watch as humans enjoyed its forbidden yumminess right in front of me, I planned my epic revenge.

I dedicated weeks of my life to research, strategizing, and staking out the ingredients cupboard, before eventually seizing the opportunity to pull off the *Great Cake Heist*.

It was an otherwise ordinary afternoon, and my humans were preparing for their weekly shopping ritual, when a freshly baked sponge emerged from the fiery depths of the range. They awaited the cake's decline into cooler temperatures, then the baking specialist smothered the cake's lower half with jam and cream before slapping the upper half onto it. I feigned indifference as I wandered nonchalantly around the kitchen. Moments before they exited the building, the baking specialist sprinkled white powder over the cake, covered it with tinfoil, then shoved it to the furthest recesses of the counter where I could no longer observe it.

The second I heard the distant thrum of a vehicle trundling into the distance, I commenced my heist.

Those fools played right into my paws, as I expected them to plant the cake 'out of reach', though I'd been practicing for the leap onto the counter by leaping onto their high-level beds whenever they were out (*they usually lifted me onto their beds, owing to my short legs*). I also pushed my springy, plush bed against the base of the counter, for better bounce.

Three attempts in, I toyed with giving up my endeavour, as every bounce seemed fated to fail. Though I refused to let adversity prevail, I dug deep into my courage reserves, and I persisted. By the fifth attempt, I was clinging onto the counter by my front paws, yet somehow found the strength to haul myself up. *I'd done it.*

Although the next obstacle was a challenging one, I'd been secretly working with foil found in the bin and hiding the evidence behind the bathtub for a while, so I had gained the skills to manipulate its shape. Working as precisely as possible, I gripped the very top of the foil dome with my front teeth and I lifted it off the cake ever so gently. After placing the foil carefully to the side, I paused to inhale the essence of its sweet aromas.

First, I scooped the jam and cream mixture from the middle of the cake with my tongue until the top half of the cake began to tilt. Second, I opened my jaw as wide as it'd go, and I sunk my teeth into the airlike sponge to gather the largest possible chunks. Finally, I reached the lower half of the cake, which combined the lightness of the vanilla sponge, the silkiness of the cream, and the fruitiness of the jam – I couldn't have imagined a more heavenly combination if I'd tried.

Despite the immense effort it took to demolish two layers of spongey cake with a rich, sugary filling, I'm not ashamed to say I was incredibly proud that I'd achieved the seemingly impossible and I'd finished the cake, in its entirety, by myself (*a feat I've never seen humans accomplish*).

However, in my excitement at accessing such an illicit indulgence, I'd accidentally got jammy paw prints all over the kitchen counter. Instead of panicking, I judiciously returned the domed tin foil to its original position, and I licked every speck of jam from the counter.

As if destiny had a sense of humour, I'd barely finished clearing the counter of jam and sponge debris when I heard the heart-stopping jangle of keys in the front door.

Swiftly as I could, I leapt from the counter, landing safely on my cushioned bed before scrabbling off it to push it back to its usual position beside the fridge.

As my humans burst into the kitchen, I was licking the last remnants of jam from my paws. They didn't discover the cake was missing until later that evening, when they were about to serve it after dinner. Confusion was written across their perplexed faces, which were scrunched in thought as they considered every angle of possibility as to their missing cake.

The closest my humans ever came to knowing the truth about what happened to their cake that day was when they blamed the cat, who then stared intently at me. Not one of my humans could comprehend my ability to reach that kitchen counter, less launch onto it for the sake of a heist – especially with such a rotund frame (*after eating all that cake, I didn't move far from my bed for about a week*).

Contributor #64
Labrador

I am part of an elite group of fortunate dogs who are trained to help humans navigate the world. It is an important job, and I love the adventures my human and I enjoy together.

There are, however, various caveats attached to a role with such weighty responsibilities, like guiding my human safely onto buses and toileting on command.

Usually, my human's attention is focused entirely on my signals and vice versa. Our actions are so synchronised that we can achieve almost anything. However, there was one occasion that our synchronicity was our downfall.

Sun blazed through the conservatory windows, casting a spell of warmth across the tiles and kitchen beyond. My human had just placed my breakfast on the kitchen floor near the conservatory, when the doorbell rang. She ordered me to continue eating and navigated her way to the front door. There was a cacophony of excited squealing and I rushed to the door, dribbling biscuits in my hurry to check my human was alright. As I arrived at the front door, my human reassured me that she was fine. Both my human and her excitable friend gave me a cuddle before they disappeared up the stairs and occupied themselves with hairdressing. Unfortunately, the interruption to my human's routine meant she wasn't available to open the door and send me outside.

So, the longer I sat beside the door, the fuller my bladder became.

Before long, my human and her friend hurried down the stairs in identical turquoise dresses that floated along behind them. Although I had remained in my usual spot beside the door, there was a beep from outside and I was harnessed for work. We jumped into a small bus that already contained four other humans in matching, flowy dresses, then we set off to an unknown destination. While I adored the extra attention I received from those around me, it was becoming increasingly difficult to sustain full control of my bodily functions.

A short time later, the bumpy bus ride came to an end, and we each stepped out onto the courtyard of a majestic castle. Our grand surroundings were so spectacular that crowds of people arrived shortly after us and began flashing cameras in our direction. Again, the additional affection as humans walked by was amazing, though my human still hadn't given me the command I desperately needed to hear.

The crowds soon disappeared into the castle, yet my human and I remained outside in the company of the humans with whom we'd travelled. I stared up at my human and whimpered a little, though she was so enthralled in conversation that I couldn't catch her attention. Although I was tempted to relieve myself there and then, a posh car rolled into the courtyard and the humans crunched their way over to greet it. From the car clambered an *enormous* sheet of shimmering material with a human trapped inside it, which caused further excitement among all the humans – including mine, who asked for us to approach the chaos.

Once the turquoise humans had each shared a cuddle and a cry with the one concealed within endless folds of white material, and they'd all smushed my face between their hands so they could kiss my forehead, they lined up at the castle doors. The human in white walked in front of my human and me, my human's friend walked beside us, and the others moved in two lines behind us.

By that point, I was on the verge of explosion, and that slow waltz down the aisle *did not* help my situation.

My human and I took our place behind the human around which the glittering material cascaded, and a slow-speaking elderly human began prattling on as I struggled to sit still.

The expanse of pristine material strewn across the stone floor in front of me was a reminder of the 'puppy pads' I used during training. So, while humans around us were occupied by the talking sloth, the urgency of my condition was so overwhelming that I had no choice but to 'release the tension'.

It took a few seconds for the humans to realise what I'd done, though looking back, the visual contrast of bright yellow spreading slowly across immaculate white material was hard to miss. My human was unaware of what I'd done to begin with, as was the human taken hostage by the vast pile of white material. I admit, I almost expected a wholly positive reaction, given that I'd likely saved a human from drowning in all that material. However, the reaction to my actions began its existence as shock, quickly evolving into panic, followed later by amusement.

Since that event, my human has never failed to follow my routine.

Contributor #67
Collie cross

If you're born on a farm, it's practically a given that you follow in your parents' paws, as you learn their job from them before passing it on to your own pups. However, I'm not like them; I *am not* gifted in the art of herding sheep…

On my first day as a sheepdog, I accidentally sent half the flock over the hill into a housing estate, and subsequently demolished several gardens in an attempt to retrieve them. My second day on the job wasn't any better, as two rogue sheep split from the flock. As I tried to herd the rogue sheep back to the others, I didn't see a small pond over a hill, and they plopped into it; the farmer wasn't best pleased when I returned with two waterlogged sheep.

Shortly after the pond incident, the farmer re-homed me to a competitive agility home. While my fellow canines were excited by the prospect of jumping over poles, weaving through sticks, climbing onto platforms at speed, and whizzing through scary tunnels, the job didn't hold much appeal for me. Despite my reservations, I did enjoy getting wrapped up in the atmosphere and found myself bouncing and barking at the human alongside the others. I liked to listen too, so training was a doddle.

The human was *extremely* impressed by my speed and precision, and it wasn't long before I was entered into a competition. Upon arrival at the venue, I felt the heaviness of pressure in the air as other dogs and humans psyched themselves up to prepare for the upcoming obstacle course. As we entered the arena, I was overwhelmed by the dozens of humans watching my every move. During that competition I let stage-fright get the better of me and didn't perform to my best – in fact, we got eliminated because I ran into the tunnel and froze partway through; I was certain a monster lurked at the other end (*turned out to be a judge*). Despite the sticky start, I continued to excel during training, which inspired the human to enter me into a second competition.

There was an epically long journey to that second competition venue, and I was fast asleep when we arrived. Apparently, we were running late, as I wasn't even given breakfast before I was dressed for competition and expected to perform. The wait for competitors to complete the course before us gave me the opportunity to have a quick snooze, as I ignored the pandemonium happening around me with dogs and humans barking incessantly at each other. Once our turn finally came around, the human seemed embarrassed by my lack of energy and was especially mean.

I wasn't prepared to be shouted at and forced around a taxing agility course without having had breakfast first, so, when we reached the platform obstacle, I curled up on it and fell back to sleep. While my nap was swiftly disturbed by the human repeatedly calling my name, that was the last time I was ever expected to compete at agility.

If I'm being honest, I truly feel that in order to be great at a job you must have a passion for it (*or at least time to eat breakfast first*); it was just taking me longer than other dogs to find a job that brought me joy.

Luckily, the third place to which I was re-homed offered me the ideal role! I am now, officially, a professional seat warmer.

I'm no longer expected to run for hours on end, in all weathers, through muddy terrain, nor am I expected to have endless energy to whiz around agility courses (*when I'd rather eat my meals in peace and nap whenever I want*). Now, my main purpose is to warm seats for my new human family. They don't care that I'm a terrible sheepdog or awful agility competitor, all they ask is that I keep their seats warm so they can vegetate in comfort. Daily walks are at least two hours long, and they're so leisurely that *I* get to decide whether to be excited by a tennis ball. I get fed hearty meals twice a day and I get *all* the cuddles – my life is perfect.

Contributor #68
Great Dane

Today, I'd like to use this time to voice my opinion on the disparity between dogs and cats.

Humans have an unsavoury relationship with cats, by allowing themselves to be manipulated by an evil they can't seem to detect.

There are *so many* examples of human favouritism towards felines, though here I'm going to address the most flagrant cases I've observed…

The cat struts around our house like he owns it. My humans could be relaxing on the sofa, when the cat suddenly brings it upon himself to force them out of his way by brutally clawing their legs until they get up! I regularly try to sit on the sofa with my humans – not to force them off it – and that's usually met with a chorus of groans before they push me away. Then, there's the furniture violations, in which the cat scags his claws down the curtains without complaint from my humans, but I accidentally eat a beanie hat one time and all of a sudden, *I'm* 'naughty'? They got their hat back the next day, *and* it was still intact; but that cat has ruined four curtains in a year and is *never* punished. Nor is the cat punished for pooping in the bathroom sandbox. Whenever I use the sandbox in the garden (*can't fit onto the one beside Toilet*), my humans are absolutely horrified and send me to 'think about my actions' while they clean it up – at least the small humans found it amusing.

Let's not forget about the 'gifts' he brings them, either. It doesn't seem to matter how gross or dead creatures are when he presents them, the cat's offerings to my humans are accepted and taken straight outside to feed Bin (*the giver of leftovers*). Sometimes, the cat brings in poor, maimed creatures that are still alive and give my humans the run-around before they die or are released back into the garden for the cat to catch again. Several times, the cat's brought slabs of raw meat from other humans' kitchens (*from what I can smell*) to flop onto the kitchen doormat, and other times he brings my humans items they already have, like sponges and socks. Whenever I bring humans my toys, they throw them away. It doesn't matter how many attempts I make to give my humans fun gifts I like to play with that I think they'll enjoy; it's never well received. And that morning I presented them with a pretty – very alive – slug on the breakfast table, they were horrified and flung the poor thing into the garden, only for a bird to swoop down and eat him!

Finally, it's highly unfair that the cat has *his own* entrance and exit door in the kitchen.

To taunt me, the cat will swagger into the house and back out again while I'm patiently – but excitedly – awaiting my humans to be ready for my daily walks. So, I decided to use the cat's 'special' door when my humans were taking too long to be ready for walkies. I poked my nose through without trouble, though by my ears I was having second thoughts. Three humans and a power saw later, I'm banned from approaching the kitchen door without humans present, while that cat can still wander in and out as he pleases.

Contributor #70
Springer Spaniel

Jobs are *very* important. Everyone has a job. *My* job is to help my human detect potent scents that are usually hidden in strange places. I love my job, but– BALL! *Sorry, work-related tic.* It can be difficult to switch-off and relax after a long day. I've noticed that my human– BALL! *Again, sorry.* My human struggles to relax after work too, and she always seems full of tension.

In fact, most of the humans I meet through– BALL! *Sorry.* Most of the humans I meet are stressed out, too. I'm certain that humans would feel better if they found something to do that makes them happy.

For example, my human doesn't allow me to have my work ball while out on walks at home– BALL! *My apologies. Where was I?* Ah, yes, walks from home. I make my out-of-work walks more fun by chasing other dogs' toys. While that sometimes seems to stress my human out more, I know that getting rid of her excess anxious energy helps her to sleep better at night.

While work can be addictive and difficult to let go– BALL! *As you can see.* Allowing work to steal your whole life will cause problems. It's important to have lots more fun and work less. *Life is supposed to be fun*!

Contributor #72
Golden Retriever cross

On my travels with my super awesome human, I've noticed a distinct lack of dogs in human workplaces, shops, and schools.

I believe humans are stressed and miserable most of the time because they aren't allowed to take their best friends everywhere.

I'm lucky because I get to visit places other dogs don't see – my human travels around in a wheeled chair and cannot reach some items or access certain doors without my support. However, I've noticed how much happier my human is to have me accompany them at work than humans who don't have their best friend with them. So, I make an effort to nuzzle and greet *every* person I meet, because I sense they're calmer and more content for a minute or two before they (*reluctantly*) walk away.

Another reason I argue *all* humans should be allowed to have a dog accompany them anywhere is the fact I've lost count of the number of humans I've seen trip over their own feet, walk through puddles in sandals, and cross roads without checking for vehicles. If these humans could have their trusted dog by their side, mistakes like that wouldn't happen anymore and the human world would be safer.

Contributor #74
Jack Russell cross

My tale is harrowing. I advise you to proceed with caution…

The vet's was a place I liked to visit, once upon a time. Despite the scratchy needles, the checking of my teeth, and listening to my internal music with those cold headphone things, the vet would give me a treat and I'd go home. Little did I know vets are capable of the most heinous of crimes.

It was a rainy Tuesday in April (*I'm assuming, based on human conversations I overheard that day*), and I was shuttled to the vet's place. Despite the oddly early hour, I didn't suspect the evil awaiting me just around the corner.

Foolishly, I regarded the vet with my usual brand of excitedness, which is the moment I should have realised something wasn't right. Unbeknown to me, my human had handed my lead to the vet above my head, then they left!

I'd never been left at the vet's place before, so I cried and howled after my human, as I assumed it was some sort of mistake. I've been living my life, since that day, in the belief that my human couldn't have known what the vet was about to do – *I sincerely hope that's true.*

They carried me through some heavy swinging doors and shoved me into a small metal cage lined with blankets and puppy pads. I continued to cry for my human, though I was doubtful they could hear me.

Then, a short while later, the vet's best friend – I think her name was 'Nurse' – carried me through to a tiled room that smelled of chemicals and human sweat, where there were a lot of wires and beeping machines.

Terrified the vet and their best friend, Nurse, were about to transform me into a robot, I wriggled and squirmed beneath Nurse's surprisingly strong hands. Although I managed to knock a few noisy metal trays onto the floor, I couldn't fight off the vet as they sunk a needle into the front of my paw.

I have no memory of what happened while I was asleep. All I know is I woke to a dry mouth, a satellite dish attached to my collar, and a throbbing between my hind legs that wasn't there before. Confused and craving chicken, I was surprised when Nurse opened the cage door and plonked me onto the floor, expecting me to stand. My legs were trembling the same way jelly wobbles on a plate, and I struggled to hold my head up with the weight of the satellite dish.

After I'd managed to stand with my legs splayed out to stop the shaking, Nurse returned me to the cage and offered me some food with a bowl of water. I may have been confused and slightly uncomfortable, but I wasn't about to turn down free food.

A short while later, my human returned to collect me. They seemed elated that I was alright, and they were horrified at the sight of the plastic, ice cream-less cone strapped around my neck. It was obvious in that moment that I'd been dog-napped, and I was furious that I couldn't snap at the vet for whatever they'd done to me. The journey home was testing, as every bump in the road sent a jolt of sharp pain along my hind legs.

It wasn't until I was lifted out of the car and expected to walk the final few steps to the front door that I realised exactly what had happened to me. *There was a breeze where there shouldn't have been a breeze.*

As soon as we got through the front door, I frantically crashed around the house in an attempt to view my 'situation'. But, unfortunately, thanks to the plastic funnel encased around my head, I couldn't see a thing. I did, however, smash a couple of lamps, crack into my human's shins, and very nearly push TV off its stand in my haste to learn the truth.

Days later, twinges of pain morphed into an uncontrollable, burning itch that I just couldn't scratch. It didn't matter how enthusiastically I lay on the living room rug and drag my tummy along; the itch *would not* go away. I took to following my human everywhere – and I mean *everywhere* – in the hope they'd save me from the ordeal I was suffering, though it didn't matter how many times I watched them bathe, my human refused to remove the cone of shame. In a last-ditch attempt to get them to help me, I raced out to the garden while it was raining and I sat upright, staring despondently into the sky as I imagined a time I wasn't itchy or without my dignity.

While I watched blobs of rain descend into my stinging eyes and felt the cold grit of reality splash against my face, I realised it wasn't my human who could fix this mess, it was the vet.

Thankfully, my dramatic performance – and cone slowly filling with rainwater – was enough to persuade my human to return me to the scene of the crime, so I could face my arch nemesis and force them to undo their damage.

It seemed my noisy entrance into the building had frightened the vet, since it was Nurse who saved me from the itchiness. Unfortunately, she couldn't return that which the vet had so callously stolen. That first lick after 'it' happened was devastating. I'd never felt so incomplete. It was sad; I didn't even get chance to say goodbye. From then, I vowed vengeance for the theft of my prized puppy potatoes.

Contributor #75
Yorkshire Terrier

I take my job *very* seriously. Humans are terrible at guarding their own territory, so I took it upon myself to protect them.

My experience as a stray, and the fact I survived an *entire* year in kennels, has given me an edge on the humans. After all, humans never put themselves in lonely kennels that require a certain toughness to survive – the humans I live with get antsy if their TV time is interrupted; they wouldn't last *a day* in kennels.

The worst thing humans can do is allow strangers into their territory, yet my humans do so regularly. Of my *many* triumphs in the months I have lived with the new human pack, the ultimate has to be what my humans refer to as 'the pizza incident'. It was late, skies outside were dark, and the humans were settled quietly into their saggy sofas for their coveted TV time. Then, the doorbell rang unexpectedly, startling the humans, causing them to jump up and rush around frantically in search of weapons to fend off the intruder. As they rallied around with those round discs they store in the food room, I raced to the door just as a human opened it. He may have been presenting them with a box that smelled incredible, but there was something I couldn't trust about that particular intruder as his outstretched hand crossed my threshold. So, I launched at him and managed to grab hold of a zip dangling from the front of his leg warmers. I held on as tightly as possible, while the creature squealed unnaturally and span around wildly in an attempt to detach me. The lovely smelling box was flung high into the air as the intruder danced about in terror. There was a brief moment I worried I'd lose grip when the zip slid down and my back paws scraped the ground, but I held fast. Thankfully, the new humans realised what I was doing and grabbed hind legs to help pull me harder, causing the intruder to cry. That tussle continued until I ripped material from the intruder's leg warmers, by which time he stumbled his way back to his noisy bike and meandered up the road as fast as he could. Ever since that day, strangers who brandish delicious-smelling boxes stand behind the gate to my threshold during interactions with the humans.

There is a form of intrusion I seem to be engaged in constant battle with, however, and that is the front door hole. Even though my humans have blocked the front door hole with a gold flap, things *still* get shoved through it almost every day. I ensure the humans are safe by shredding *anything* pushed into my territory. Sometimes it angers them, but I know humans will realise it's for their own good, eventually.

Contributor #78
Staffordshire Bull Terrier

More often than not, humans would see the scars across my head and immediately seek to avoid me at all costs. I *wish* I could have explained to them that those scars are from a previous human owner who hurt me and not from fighting. I was grateful when there was a human family who saw beyond those scars and brought me into their home. There were other dogs who'd arrive then leave on a regular basis, rarely staying longer than a few weeks, so I feared these kind humans might send me back to kennels too. That was when I realised I had to befriend the whole family and not just the human who fed me. But there was an issue – the leader human (*the one who fed me*) would not allow dogs near her pups. We could watch the pups play through windows, and I longed for nothing more than to join in with their games.

In the time I'd spent in the humans' home, I watched them carefully to learn a map of the territory. That exercise proved useful when I noticed a human pup clambering onto the kitchen counters without their adult around. I was afraid the tiny human might fall and injure themselves, so I ran to the gate separating the pups from us, and I jumped over it before running, as quickly as I could, into the kitchen. I didn't want to bark and startle the little one, so I followed their path along the counter and positioned myself beneath the area onto which they were most likely to fall. As I'd anticipated, the small human slipped on the smooth counter's edge and tumbled off it just as their adult entered the room. I was glad to have been of service, as the pup landed squarely on my back, sending my entire body slamming upon the cold tile of the kitchen floor. While the youngster was perfectly uninjured, I had to be rushed to the vets for a broken hip. I would experience that pain and endure the surgery all over again if it meant I could save a human from getting hurt.

After that day, I became a permanent fixture in the human family, and I was the only canine allowed to stay. I was also given a meaningful role as 'healing dog', for which I got to visit schools, and hospitals, and care homes, and any other place where humans required some extra cuddles to cheer them up. Through my new role, I am constantly learning about humans, and I listen to every word they say.

However, there are disadvantages to working with young humans, most namely their issues of self-control; I cannot count the occasions I've suffered a sticky finger up the nose. *Yet I love what I do*!

HORSES

Contributor #81
Welsh Section D

Working for a riding school has its challenges, the biggest of which is dealing with anxious riders. As 'fright or flight' creatures, humans tend to react to situations they deem 'scary' in two different ways; they either turn to face whatever it is they're frightened of and try scaring it away with their frail brand of courage, or they leg it.

I've tried *every* method under the sun to coax humans through stressful scenarios. Throwing them into the things they're scared of doesn't work – especially if the things they fear happen to be walls or puddles. Simply walking past, through, under, or over whatever they're afraid of isn't effective either, as it makes them lazy and unable to tackle obstacles by themselves. And don't get me started on waiting for humans to calm down *before* tackling whatever it is that's bothering them, because that extends jumping lessons far beyond reasonable parameters.

The best way to work with humans is to use empathy. For example, if a rider tenses at the sight of, say, plastic bags, I tense with them. Unless the rider stays calm, I spook at speed until they learn not to fret over the little things.

Contributor #82
Piebald Cob cross

'Monotonous' is the word I'd use to describe my previous job. Of course, I was amazing at the job, a legend in trekking circles as many would say, but there's only so much side-kicking, mouth-jabbing, and mind-numbing chatter it's possible to endure before one's zest for life is well and truly stripped from them. That was me.

The newbies *always* selected me as their steed thanks to my sturdy frame and long, wavy mane. I made them look great in pictures and I never threw them into the sea – no matter how irritating they were. That was until one scorching summer morning when an ignorant human declared themselves capable of sending me off-course, despite having spent less than two minutes in the saddle, *ever*.

Trailing behind the others, I sensed my rider was a loner and disinterested in fellow humans. So, I went along with the human's suggestion to try a different path, for a laugh. We seemed to have found a refreshingly cool trail that was shaded by an archway of trees. I was beginning to have a nice time when the stupid human spotted a pool of water and jumped out of the saddle to 'have a quick paddle'. Turns out that 'inviting shallow pool' was a deep lagoon. The human splooshed under the water but didn't emerge. Bubbles rising and popping at the surface indicated exactly where the silly human was, so I shook my head madly until the reins flew over my head before approaching the water's edge.

I stood still, reins sending a rippling across the water's surface, for what seemed a *very* long time. Then, miraculously, the human's head popped up out of the water, coughing and choking, before reaching for my reins. My goodness were they heavy, and my tongue was almost sliced off in the process, but I managed to drag the sopping creature out of the lagoon and rolled her on her side as she had a brief panic attack. Not wanting to leave the human unattended – there were predatory squirrels lurking everywhere – I sent a call for help from the depths of my lungs. It wasn't too long before other humans heard my booming voice and rescued the ridiculous human, who made a full recovery and would visit me regularly afterwards (*for hugs, not trekking*).

My life transformed drastically after that incident, and I was promoted to a prestigious role within the mounted police force! No two days are the same anymore. I wake up every morning raring to get out and patrol a different route. Sometimes, it's the seemingly weird, unexpected events that permit the best changes.

Contributor #83
Dutch Warmblood cross

As a professional eventer, I work tirelessly to stay at the top of my field (*pun intended*). I am surrounded by a team of humans who ride and train me, and a separate team who groom me, bathe me, feed me, muck-out my stable, turn me out into the field, or monitor my appointments with health care professionals (*vets, physios, farriers, and the like*). Best of all, each and every one of those humans instinctively knows how fortunate they are to be in my presence.

Although, being rated one of the industry's greatest athletes does come with its drawbacks, most notably, that humans can't get enough of me. I find myself having to wade through crowds of them en route to *every* competition phase. I feel for those humans occasionally, I really do, as they obviously aren't able to interact with incredible horses, such as myself, in their everyday lives. It is a travesty that not all humans have access to horses. *However*, I will make the argument that humans, as a species, are in the strongest position – ecologically speaking – to advance themselves. I used to be certain they could find better ways to spend their time, instead of chasing me down and tugging my tail as I enter

the arena for a dressage test, or slapping my
neck when I'm about to embark on the cross-
country course, but, in observing those humans
more closely, it was revealed that they are
trapped by mediocrity. I *cannot fathom* how
humans get anywhere near their desired levels of
success when they're expected to answer to
other humans whose concern for them is non-
existent.

Consider the hierarchy of various breeds
of human I encounter at events; there's 'judges',
the 'riders', the 'watchers', and the 'helpers'.

'Judges' reside in the upper echelons of
control, positioning themselves out of harm's
way, in a cosy environment, as they preside over
the fate of all those beneath them in the
hierarchy. While they have the power to cause
ecstatic displays of celebration, they're also
responsible for the grumbling grief of
devastation if a competitor fails. Despite
knowing nothing of the world beyond
themselves, these judges control the actions of
'riders', 'watchers', *and* 'helpers'. I, for one,
would hold a deeper respect for the judges'
position of authority if they could prove
themselves worthy of the accolade at every level
of the hierarchy. I'm certain it would be an
enlightening experience for a judge to complete
a one-day event successfully without incident,
muck-out a stable in those fancy outfits, or

replace a fallen show-jump in the rain; only then, once they understand *every* perspective, should they be allowed to judge others.

'Riders' are perhaps in the most privileged position of all, since not only do they get to work with remarkable horses, but they also don't hold responsibility for 'watchers' and 'helpers'. Yet, riders do possess the power to order others around if they wish.

'Watchers' include those previously mentioned humans who migrate in crowds.

'Helpers' have the worst deal. They are forced to work under terrible conditions, lugging around heavy jump poles, clearing the arena of droppings, and putting up with inflated rider egos. The look on helpers' faces when they observe a hot beverage approaching is both heart-warming and a little sad. It seems those poor humans work harder than the rest, taking care of others without concern for themselves.

Therefore, to conclude my findings, I truly believe that humans should be gifted the opportunity to observe conditions for all in the hierarchy – and I also think helpers deserve better catering facilities as well as nicer, waterproof, shelters while working outside. My closing statement about humans: *they are naturally unsuited to the task of dominance or judgement, without first understanding the perspective of their lowliest helper.*

Contributor #86
Thoroughbred

In another life, I thundered to victory through finishing posts while soaring upon the metaphorical tidal wave of applause. I can recall the heart-thumping anticipation, the face-melting speeds, and the whip-cracking pressure of racing like it was yesterday. Alas, my life is *far* different now. I've swapped the track for the arena, and a string of jockeys for one – very opinionated – human with a fear of water trays. I have become an amateur's show jumper.

My racing days may be long gone, though my reputation for being fiery on the track has seeped into the consciousness of the local community, who flee when they see me approaching. While my human adores the fact we're never expected to fight for space in the collecting ring or endure small talk with other riders, I can't help but feel hurt by the notion that humans assume I'm incapable of change.

Take an event I attended just last week as a prime example of the misjudgement I'm forced to endure…

It was a glorious day, the sun was blazing on my back as it sent a warmth to the tips of my hooves, the grass was luscious (*and within reach*), and the showground was bustling.

Then, once my human had tacked me up, clambered into the saddle, and we trotted towards the collecting ring, there was a flurry of panic as humans almost tripped over themselves to clear a path for me.

As if being treated as a scary dragon in the collecting ring wasn't insulting enough, when I happened to spook at a plastic bag rattling in the breeze as I exited the arena, the human holding the plastic bag dramatically threw himself to the ground, throwing his arms in front of his face in terror!

I was more riled up than ever as we approached the show jumping course. In the old days I might've taken my anger out on the nearest human – a stomach kick here, an arm bite there – but I've changed, and I chose to channel my frustrations into the course. If it weren't for my human's infernal yanking of the reins and ungainly unplanned dismount into the water jump, I'd have scored a clear round.

While my human tied me to the side of the trailer so she could hide inside it to change back into her usual untidies, I watched the showground around me and was shocked at what I saw. A Shetland pony, no taller than my knees, was being prepped for a showing class. All seemed calm until a miniature human was secured in the pony's saddle.

The creature seemed possessed, as he decided the perfect time for throwing a random, vertical buck was as the small human leaned down to pat him!

Kudos to the little human for clinging on tightly enough to stay on board, though I was extremely disappointed in its adults for not taking the young human away from that dangerous Shetland.

Tensions subsided surprisingly quickly, as other humans approached to coo and marvel at that monster of a pony. It didn't matter that he was surrounded by a herd of humans, the Shetland quickly tired of being admired and started to scrape at the long grass with his teeny tiny hoof. The humans were too enthralled in their admiration of him to notice the signal, and the mini human atop the pony was busy gazing at a butterfly fluttering past them. I did call to the group, in an attempt to warn them of the Shetland's impending tantrum, but they stared at me and took my behaviour as a request for them to move slowly away.

Unfortunately for the little human, the Shetland utilised the command to walk forwards as an excuse to dart sideways, startle his handler – who he subsequently lost to a slip on cow pat – and charge around the field at a flat-out gallop. By this point, I could sense the small human would've been better off bailing, because that

Shetland had something wicked planned. Whether through courage or complacency, the young human continued to cling onto the saddle for dear life, which angered the pony. Without warning, the Shetland swooped his muzzle to the grass 'for a quick graze' and his startled rider flew over his ears at speed.

Luckily, the little one landed on their cushioned behind and bounced a few times, unhurt, before bursting into tears. I fully expected the humans to shoot hate at that Shetland, who was grazing contentedly with reins wrapped around his head while his miniature rider was bawling. Yet I was wrong. The moment that young one had been comforted to a state of quiet sobbing, the adult returned them to the pony's saddle and set off for their class. Then, to add insult to injury, that Shetland was surrounded by a symphony of adoration wherever he went, as humans flocked to pet his fuzzy coat and scruffle his fluffy mane. Worst of all, the pony didn't even like having all that attention – he just wanted to munch grass. *What's up with that?!*

Contributor #94
Anglo-Arabian Horse

I've owned my current human for approaching
sixteen years. While it took a while to nudge
them into shape, I can finally say that I am the
proud owner of a fully trained Homo Sapien.

My secrets to unlocking human potential
rely on a balanced concoction of behaviour
modification and positive reinforcement.

First, I wanted to address my human's
poor understanding of time. The timing of my
human's arrival with my breakfast feed was
abysmal, as she'd saunter onto the yard
whenever suited her. Then, my human had the
audacity to stand in the centre of the yard
'chatting' to other humans, as she carelessly
dangled my ready-prepared feed bucket by one
handle and allowed crumbs to drop to the floor.
I tried neighing to get her attention, though that
didn't work – she'd shoot a 'that is cute but I'm
busy' glance over her shoulder at me, then
continue her conversation as if her noble steed
wasn't dying of starvation ten feet away. Then, I
took to pacing my stable. The thought behind
pacing my stable was to destroy my once
immaculate shavings bed, in the hope she'd
realise the error of her ways and feed me faster
in future if she didn't want to waste her efforts

to keep my stable clean. But that plan didn't work either. So, I evolved my techniques based on my human's behaviour, and chose to kick my stable door as loudly as possible until she brought my breakfast to me. To begin with, kicking my stable door engaged little more than a 'shut up, will you? I'm talking' glare, followed by a threat to shove something somewhere or other. It wasn't until another human complained to my human about the racket I was making that my human hastily trotted my breakfast over to me. Following on that roaring success, I took what I'd learned – that humans care *a lot* more about other humans' perceptions of them than about their own interests – and I continued to batter my stable door every morning until I was fed. Soon enough, my human had received *so many* complaints about my door-kicking that she'd arrive on time without fail.

That first lesson was so effective, however, that I had to resort to an entirely new lesson as my human would rush tacking me up and wrench the girth so high so quickly that I felt I'd split in two! Sometimes, she'd yank the girth with such force and enthusiasm that she'd punch herself in the face. Owing to my discomfort and her self-injuring behaviours, I declared it appropriate to teach my human the importance of adjusting the girth step by step. It began with a trick I learned while I was doing hard time at a riding school for ditching my previous human in a river, and that trick was called the 'girth reliever'. To perform the 'girth reliever' trick, I needed to pretend to eat my hay nonchalantly as I'd fill my lungs with air and slowly pushed my sides out as far as they could go. The gradual expansion of my girth area went unnoticed, as my human faffed about with her mobile phone. My human foolishly believed I'd put on weight overnight as she huffed and puffed while struggling to tighten the girth, when in reality, all she'd done is tired herself out. We set off on our leisurely hack with a couple of other horse and rider combinations from the yard, and all seemed to be well. As the humans rode us towards the infamous local canter track, my jogging caused the saddle to start bobbing about a bit – though my human was so deep in conversation with another rider that she didn't notice. Just as we reached the start of the canter track, I was impressed with my standing start as I raced to overtake my field-mate. However, the faster I was galloping around the corner, the more the saddle was slipping. Before long, the saddle tipped to the right and my human was dangling at my side, desperately grasping at my wispy mane to pull herself and the saddle up onto my back. It just so happened that a particularly scary bird flew out of the hedge as I slowed to a steady canter.

Unfortunately for my human, my canter to gallop transition is a little messy, especially when I'm also trying to avoid a puddle in the middle of the path, and she fell off. She missed the mucky puddle by an inch, but my human was pretty miffed that I'd cantered away with a 'thousand-pound' saddle beneath my perfectly toned stomach. Never again did my human secure the girth so abruptly my eyes felt they might pop out of my head – a big win!

Finally, I have taught my human to interpret my longing to become a – supremely handsome – field ornament instead of the county-level competitive machine she wanted me to become. There was era, long ago, when my human foolishly believed I'd become an award-winning eventer. After our first cross-country schooling trip ended in disaster – namely, a broken ankle – we moved our focus to dressage (*or rather, 'stressage' as my human now refers to it*). Flatwork seemed quite nice to begin with. There was no expectation to haul my body over solid fences and I liked being able to 'zone out' as my human worked on keeping her toes pointing upwards. Eventually, the tension that'd build in my human as she desperately tried to recall entire dressage tests seeped through the reins. Our last dressage test ended with a snapped bridle and ruined breeches. Then, we embarked on showing. I felt the boring circles and expectation to lengthen my stride on command were manageable, so my human and I did well at showing competitions for a while. Although, I wanted to get out of the 'game' before my human got too excited about the prospect of travelling more than an hour to a competition venue, so, one summer afternoon I feigned fear at a flapping rosette ribbon, reared right in front of the judge, then charged full-pelt towards the spectators, who had the foresight to dive out of my way as I jumped over the rope fence and thundered my way back to the horsebox. My human managed to stay on board, though she was rather white and wobbly by the time she mustered the energy to dismount. To prevent my human from sending me to a different human, I then transformed into the cuddliest, most loving, affectionate horse she'd ever known.

Now, my human couldn't live without me. The only expectations held by my human are to not spook, buck, or rear while out hacking, to smother my human with affection if she seems a bit miserable, and to put up with the occasional visit from her human family.

Contributor #100
Connemara cross

Overhearing your own 'for sale ad' is enough to turn anyone into a bitter, miserable husk; *not me*. I'm using this opportunity to craft a 'for sale ad' for the human I heard rehearsing the article she was creating to pass me off on the next 'child' – who inevitably turns out to be taller than the average tree and sends me packing to the next stable within a month because they've 'outgrown' my (*perfect*) petite physique.

This is the human's 'for sale ad' for me: *"Very sad sale of talented mounted games pony. Connemara cross. Gelding. 13hh. 11 years old. Always in the ribbons and quick off the mark. No vices but does kick door at feeding time. Great for farrier, vet, dentist, physio, etc. 100% to clip, travel, groom. Amazing with kids. Builds confidence in nervous and novice riders. Vetting and trial welcome. Call or text for more info."*

No idea what goats have to do with it, but that human was liberal with the truth. I hate the vet, never see the dentist without heavy sedation, and the farrier is terrified of me.

So, this is my 'for sale ad' for *that* one: *"For sale, 15-year-old mounted games fanatic. Eats too many sandwiches, not up for sharing. Probably at risk of laminitis. Height: too tall.*

Misbehaves when denied winning place at competitions. Loves vet, farrier, dentist visits; provided those with whom they're dealing are deemed 'attractive'. Not a sad sale since they pull too tightly on the reins, bounce too much on the saddle, and whine too much about losing. Vices include – but are not limited to – morning moodiness, poor hygiene, and never carrying mints. Trials welcome, provided I can watch."

Honesty is always the best policy, though I don't think there's a pony on the planet crazy enough to choose *that* human!

EXOTIC
PETS

Contributor #101
Pygmy Hedgehog

Cardboard is a taboo subject for humans. They can't understand my relationship with it, and I can't understand why it bothers them. Tubes are my favourite form of cardboard. I *love* shoving my nose into the dark abyss of cardboard tubes and snuffling around my enclosure, carefree and unencumbered by the heavy expectations of life. Humans, on the other paw, are quick to become distressed about my enjoyment of cardboard tubes and take the tubes away. I wish humans would lighten up and play with some cardboard tubes themselves, so they can learn of the great joy and enlightenment that comes from moving around one's enclosure without worrying about the outside world.

Humans love bathing, but I *do not love* it. Despite their best efforts to encourage me to enjoy being splashed with water and have my paws scrubbed with a toothbrush, I'd much prefer playing with cardboard tubes. Usually, I strike against bathing by curling into a ball and floating around the sink-tub.

Something I have in common with my humans is our love of food. My favourites are dry cat food, chicken, scrambled egg, and mealworms. Their favourites are pizza and beer.

Contributor #104
Cockatoo

They're everywhere. We can't get away from them. It won't be long until they rule the world, yet humans cannot see the threat. Humans only see what's right in front of them; they don't want to look ahead. I'm talking about *screens*. Those flashy, light-up rectangles keep humans from pursuing healthier habits, like reading, or puzzles, or hand-feeding me peanuts and pineapple all day. It's as if humans have forgotten how to have fun. My flock of humans used to spend Saturday nights playing with cards and board games. Now, my humans spend their Saturday nights munching through boxes of greasy chicken (*how offensive*) as they melt into the sofas and relinquish their minds to the TV.

I've even noticed how my humans have started to adjust their lives around the TV. It's bonkers, really, that humans are supposedly the earth's most intelligent species, but can't foresee technology evolving its own super-intelligence and taking over.

Yesterday, I protested the TV's rising power by stealing its remote. My humans still can't find it (*hilarious; they'll never find it*), and they haven't talked to each other so much in years as they have in their search of the remote!

Contributor #109
Bearded Dragon

As a recovering vegan, there was a time I'd refuse to eat food that *may* have suffered harm. Although, after a week of being unable to eat anything at all due to the thought of causing pain to innocent plants, vegetables, worms, and crickets, I resigned myself to the vet's demands and began to eat food once again.

I've never felt so healthy as the week I reintroduced food into my diet! But I've never forgotten the reason for my decision to become vegan, which is why I allow my food to die of natural causes before consuming it. Instead of hunting the crickets that ruin the ambience of my home, I wait for them to die naturally and refuse to cause them harm. The same goes for plants and vegetables, since I will only eat them if they are completely still – one flicker of a leaf and I'll walk away, no-matter how hungry I feel.

I respect all living creatures. However, I've noticed humans don't respect food in quite the same way, as they prefer other humans hunt, kill, then wrap their food in plastic sheeting prior to eating it. I'm certain humans would derive more joy from eating, say jacket potatoes, by watching them live happily in the wild first.

Contributor #110
Chameleon

It baffles me that humans are never comfortable in their own skin. While I'm flattered they seek to replicate my magnificent colour-changing abilities, a recent observation forced me to rethink the consequences of humans trying to be something they're not…

Take one of my many house humans as a prime subject: the weather was getting warmer, and they longed to bare more skin, but they were unhappy with their natural tone (*likely upon studying my powers of transformation*) and sought to change it by drastic means. They returned to the house one afternoon, and I barely recognised them – they were the most glowing shade of orange I'd ever seen! And, to make matters worse, after sitting on the pale leather sofa for a short while, they peeled themselves off it in the heat and left a body print behind that angered the other humans. The poor thing was *so* embarrassed by their failed attempt to replicate my super power, they didn't leave the house for *two weeks*.

Here's the truth of it: humans should *never* try to imitate another. Their own powers will be found if they realise how enchantingly unique they are *without* modifications.

FARM RESIDENTS

Contributor #40
Dexter Cow

Machines ruin *everything*. The only thing we hate more than machines is sheep and their stuck-up attitudes (*'oh, I'm a sheep, look at me, I can grow my own winter coat and not have to get chilly in the rain, blah'*). Our farmer used to walk the fields with his trusty canine and move our herd by waving a stick at us, then cursing at the top of his voice, before, eventually, bribing us into the barn. Though since he got that *quad bike*, he tears up the grass while chasing us about the fields and he lets the thing grumble at us, loudly, with its irritating chuckle. We're also expected to move at unreasonable speeds, now he's got that *monster* to hurry us along.

So, last week, we formed a plan to rid the farm of *that* machine once and for all. We knew our farmer would park the metal beast beside the fence as he checked the water trough, so we had a narrow window to destroy it. While Bessie took one for the team and shoved her hoof through the fence to distract our farmer, the rest of us bulldozed the bike and sent it crashing through the fence. Unfortunately, our plan backfired. The broken fence allowed *hundreds* of sheep to pile into *our* field and ruin our grazing worse than any machine could.

Contributor #41
Holstein-Friesian

Born into the milk trade, I had minimal experience of humans until I was retired to a petting zoo.

I've spent the majority of my life in and out of milking sheds, nurturing the next generation of both my species and humanity. To me, producing milk and gifting its goodness to those who need it was the most natural process in the world. Though recently, I've realised that while humans are perfectly accepting of my milk and the consumption of it, they have a bizarre perspective regarding their own milk.

My pen offers a full view of the human eating area. It's not unusual to observe humans drinking milk in their coffee, or slathering bread with butter, or even to see them get excited over an ice-cream, yet the second a human mother feeds her young using her own milk supply, there's an awkwardness in the atmosphere that creates an uncomfortable tension for the poor mother, who's doing something important by taking care of her calf.

I wonder whether humans would be more accepting of their own produce if they replaced cattle in milking sheds? Perhaps then, *all* mothers could nourish their calves in peace.

Contributor #44
Jacob Ram

Although my own humans accepted my unusual appearance, I'd been laughed out of showing competitions my whole life due to having six horns instead of the 'ideal' four horns. Because of my undesirable look, humans eliminated my ability to procreate and sent me to join a field of ewes; it was emasculating. But, I was grateful not to be sent to slaughter or worse – to an interactive farm park, *shudder* – so, I grazed my way through life, waiting for it to get better.

Then, in the middle of the night while my humans were away with the dogs, I noticed three trespassers skulking around the farmhouse. Thanks to my extra horns I'm an expert at opening gates, so, I slid the gate open quietly as possible, then sneaked through the shadows to get a closer look at what those humans were doing. I couldn't understand exactly what they were doing, though my instincts told me there was something very wrong about their behaviour. My desire to protect my humans' home was overwhelming, and I didn't stop to think before I was galloping towards the biggest one, horns pointing forwards. He squealed in pain as the tip of a horn impaled his leg. The other human turned to defend their leader,

though swiftly turned to run in the opposite
direction when I pointed my horns at them and
scraped a front foot across the gravel. To
guarantee the trespassers wouldn't return, I
chased them all the way across the farmyard and
along the driveway, until they scrambled,
terrified, into a vehicle and sped away. I then
returned to the dullness of my field, grateful that
none of the ewes had noticed the open gateway
(*I didn't fancy chasing them back into the field*).

Somehow, my humans discovered what
I'd done, and they promoted me to the coveted
position of 'guard dog'. I was allowed to roam
the farmyard freely, alongside the other guard
dogs, and many humans would visit to stand
with me and admire my six horns.

Contributor #45
Cheviot Ewe

I was raised in a human house. Humans fed me, comforted me, changed my nappy, and loved me more than life itself. Then, completely out of the blue, they released me into the field with *sheep*, of all creatures. I couldn't think of anything I might've done to upset them, which is when I realised it must've been a terrible mistake and that I needed to return home.

The funny thing about sheep is that they have this strange, uncontrollable compulsion to follow others everywhere. So, when I jumped over the fence to make my way home, the idiots decided to follow me and ended up flipping themselves upside down, getting stuck between the fence posts, or clambering successfully over only to slip into a ditch and get stranded there. I was about to slip away from the scene of woolly pandemonium when my humans arrived. Amidst the chaos, my humans failed to acknowledge my attempts to communicate, and I was chased back into the field by the dog I'd been snuggled in front of the fire with a few weeks previously.

Unperturbed by my humans' mistake, I set to work on my second plan to return home. It was time to get their attention. Therefore, I pushed my way through a dense hedge with a noisy road on the other side of it. Although it was dangerous, I hoped my daring effort to be reunited would remind my humans why they loved me so much. But, as usual, sheep ruined it. Instead of the bold escape I'd envisioned – by which putting myself in harm's way would get the attention of my humans – those darn sheep followed me *again* and put a stop to all the traffic. While I'd planned an emotional reunion with my humans, it was sad to see them so stressed and frantic as they panicked about the hundreds of sheep strewn across four lanes of a busy highway. It took twelve humans and five dogs to return the sheep to their field. Sadly, none of the humans seemed to understand my requests for them to take me back to my home.

Wishing to avoid the prying eyes of those sheep, I concocted *another* scheme to return to my humans that involved stealth. I waited until most of the sheep were asleep, then I tip-toed to the stream and quietly waded up it towards the neighbouring humans' farmhouse. I hoped to wake the neighbours, explain my situation, and ask them politely to take me home. Apparently, I wasn't quiet enough, since I was halfway up the stream when I turned to see at least fifty sheep slipping, sliding, and bowling into each other as they fought to remain upright against the gently trickling flow of water. It was too late to abandon my plan, so, on I waded.

Eventually reaching the farmhouse, accompanied by the twenty-or-so sheep who'd managed the journey, I rapped on the front door with my hoof and awaited an answer. The farmer yanked the door open, looking around angrily above my head as he brandished a shotgun. I gave him a little call, to let him know I didn't mean any harm, then he looked down at me, dropped the shotgun, rubbed his weary eyes, and called for his partner. Long story short, thanks to my loyal band of followers, I was taken back to the field with those ridiculous sheep and *not* returned to my humans.

My efforts to return home to my humans are ongoing. And I am certain I'll be living in the cosy warmth of the house just as soon as I can shake the loser flock of sheep who have apparently made me their leader.

Contributor #46
Saddleback Sow

Humans love nothing more than to feed me. They worship my curvaceous figure, praising every inch of my wonderfully blubbery frame. And yet, humans cannot accept their own natural blubber.

I reside in the grounds of the world's most spectacular castle, and I am able to observe various human archetypes every day.

The most surprising of behaviours (*and there have been numerous – I mean, to what species is it acceptable to blow smoke around others' faces?*) I have observed is their bizarre obsession with size. Of course, there are some humans who fail to follow dictated expectations, yet in general, I get the impression that humans believe themselves more worthy of admiration if their stature is small. For instance, many humans will 'pose for photos' in front of my enclosure, and instead of beholding my radiant beauty, they're hyper focused on straining, stretching, and angling their bodies to portray an abstract version of their true selves.

It is my understanding, after eight years surrounded by humans, that they could benefit from observing species other than their own in their pursuit of self-acceptance and gratitude.

ZOO
RESIDENTS

Contributor #3
Chimpanzee

For many years, I've been fascinated by that most amusing of creatures – the human.

They may roam the world 'freely' with their 'phones', their 'money', and those strangely shaped foot containers they love so much, but I am of the opinion humans have burdened themselves beyond the realm of true contentment. Take my studies as proof…

Infants are supposed to bring joy and the promise of genetic continuation, and yet, human adults accompanying their unruly infants appear in a constant state of stress. An adult's frayed demeanour concealed behind a false, toothy smile at passers-by as they attempt to bribe their young – hoping to regain a microscopic measure of control – is depressing to witness. My only reservations about human infants are their infernal glass-tapping behaviours, which give me a headache, and their insistence on squashing their snotty noses against the glass of my enclosure; otherwise, I find them charming. So, it seems to me that humans force each other to feel so guilty for procreating that they're punished for it by unrealistic expectations that infants ought to behave as adults.

Then, there's the human reaction to conflict. I've lost count of the occasions human squabbles break out in front of my enclosure – usually over viewing areas or infant behaviour – and the arguing parties raise their voices, become red-faced, then part ways even angrier. It's such a waste of time.

While I cannot influence humanity to treat their young with less oppression, I believe I can inspire a better reaction to conflict in order for them to regain some sense of contentment that has been lost on the route to 'civilised life'. My mate had longed to swing from my tyre in our shared outer enclosure for some time. Mating season was over, so the will to allow them to act irrationally had dispersed. I'm also an advocate of equal rights, and if I were swinging on their tyre, I'd expect to be ousted post-haste. As it happened, my mate paid no heed to my polite requests for them to vacate my tyre swing, and I'm not proud of it, though I did resort to vocalising my discontent. They continued to ignore my upset as they'd swing gaily back and forth in taunting smugness. I resisted the overwhelming urge to push them off, instead turning to pick a sizeable twig with which to irritate them. But, as I turned back, something smacked me so hard I fell with a thud. As I wiped faeces from my stinging eyes, I gave a respectful nod and found a different tyre.

Contributor #4
Marmoset

I used to live in a human habitat. It was always busy (*on account of the many humans who lived there too*) but it was very nice. But now, for about five years, I have been living in this zoo habitat (*with only monkeys, no humans stay*). So, I can only play with the same humans every day and I have to watch the other humans through the glass, which makes me feel sad sometimes.

I miss my humans. Anyway, it was a long, long time ago, when I was a baby, and I remembered watching my humans use the magical cold food box. There was always food in there for them, and for me. Then one day, I felt like searching for my own magical food source. That was when I found a special tree plant in the corner. No humans were about, so I bit into the thin tree, expecting to find the best-tasting sap ever. However, the sap burst from the pipe so hard that I got shot across the room to the opposite wall! In seconds, the runny tree sap had soaked the entire room and sent things fizzing with sparkly lights.

Oh, I think I *just* realised why my humans did not want me to share their habitat anymore; they wanted to keep that special, runny sap all for themselves. *Makes sense.*

Contributor #6
Elephant

Watching humans eat near my enclosure is hilarious. It's no wonder they're so small with such soft bodies. Not only do they eat tiny amounts, but they're unbelievably fussy!

Just a few days ago, I witnessed a human sneeze on another human's sandwich when they were too busy gazing at me to notice. A third human then got involved, informed the second human that the first human had sneezed on their sandwich, then the second human walked over to the nearest bin to feed it the sandwich before storming away. After that, other humans gave the first human a wide berth. However, during the feeding time event an hour or so previously, the human whose sandwich later got sneezed on had been lucky enough to hand me an apple, which I courteously scooped up with my trunk. I'm not sure whether the human was aware, but my trunk is the equivalent to a human nose, and they had no issue unwrapping a sandwich and eating it shortly after I'd wiped my trunk on their hands. Why is it acceptable to humans to interact with my trunk around food but not their own? I can't imagine that leaves much opportunity to eat if they're so disgusted by their own bodies that they must throw food away.

Then, there's the issue humans have with eating food from the ground. Where do they think their food is grown? I noticed a human drop their crisps to the ground in front of my enclosure the other day after another human barged them with a shoulder as they walked past. Instead of simply picking up the crisps and eating them, the human stared despondently at the ground for a moment, before scooping the crisps into their hands and feeding them – crinkly packet and all – to the bin. Bearing in mind that, again, the very same human had watched me scoop food from the ground to eat and had been fascinated by my behaviour.

Another reason I believe humans are so tiny is their strange habit of eating for barely half an hour each day. I need to be eating for at least seventeen hours a day (*there's a clock on the inner wall of my covered enclosure, so, naturally, I've learned about and monitored time in the interests of factuality*). Surely, it's basic instinct to eat when hungry? Although, it helps me understand humans a bit better; because if I didn't eat whenever I felt hungry, I'd probably be an angry little mammal, too.

Contributor #8
Rhinoceros

As a calf, humans chased me away from my mother and I never saw her again. A different group of humans discovered me three sunsets later, collapsed and exhausted.

It was a terrifying time. They wrapped up my eyes so I couldn't see, and they blocked my ears so I couldn't hear. I called and called to my mother; she was my whole world, and I was so frightened not knowing where she was or if she was alright. I decided I hated humans.

Once the humans had removed the wrapping from my eyes and had unblocked my ears, all I wanted to do was charge at them. I was infuriated to be away from my mother, and I blamed those humans for keeping me away from her. No matter how many bottles they fed me or how hard they tried to interact, I wanted nothing to do with humans.

Then, I became unwell. In fact, I was so unwell I could barely move. To my surprise, after charging at them and threatening to headbutt their knees, the humans cared for me continuously for many moon cycles. Gradually, I gained strength and recovered from the illness – thanks to the humans. I warmed to them, as the humans made attempt after attempt to bond.

They would talk to me calmly and feed me bottles, before stroking my ears with their soft hands as I dozed. Soon afterwards, I realised I was safe with the humans and I began to enjoy my time with them. They'd take me outside to run, prance, and roll in mud with them. I'd leap and bound along a lengthy pathway, leaving dust clouds wherever I charged. I enjoyed making humans laugh, it was a happy sound.

There was a cushioned area in the corner of my enclosure where the humans would rest and invite me to join them. I liked to snuggle next to the humans; while they could never replace her, their closeness and devotion reminded me of my mother.

Imagining I'd be alone with the humans forever, it was a pleasant surprise when they released me to a vast enclosure filled with endless foliage and mud baths ready for wallowing. That's where I met the one who would later become my mate. It was wonderful, seeing another just like me for the first time since I lost my mother.

My health continued to improve in leaps and bounds, along with my co-ordination, until it was time to bring a calf of our own into the world. Without the care and dedication of the good humans who saved my life, my calf wouldn't be here today.

If a human causes harm to you, that doesn't mean all humans are unkind. It is vital you don't give up on humanity, because finding the right humans to surround yourself with will transform your life for the better, *I promise*.

Contributor #13
Python

Addiction can be a bit of a problem, especially if you're addicted to doing something others may deem 'spiteful'. My addiction relates to humans; namely, terrifying them.

I came across my addiction completely by accident early one morning, when the new keeper left my enclosure open. Having lived a mundane existence for the first seven years of my life at the zoo, little did I know I was about to embark on an adventure that'd provide pleasure for the next thirteen years (*and counting*). My preference for damp environments led me to a mysterious room where water pooled in shiny, white bowls. I slithered into one on a whim, hoping the water would be refreshingly warm, only to find the water to be uncomfortably chilly. However, upon sliding back out of the bowl, a human was stood, frozen, in front of me. I froze too, and we stared at each other for a moment before they screamed in a painfully high pitch and raced out of the open entranceway. Suddenly, a spark tingled the length of my body (*though, admittedly, it could've been the vibrations from that human's scream*), and I followed the human's scent until I was caught by a keeper.

Determined not to get caught again, I had to wait a few months for my next escape. That time I chose a different environment and curled tightly around a tree branch overhanging a bustling pathway full of humans. Although most of the passing humans didn't look up, stretching down and startling one or two of them with a well-timed hiss was enough to cause a frenzy of panic as humans scrambled over each other to get away from me. An extra bonus of that particular hiding place was that keepers couldn't reach me without a ladder – gifting me an extra couple of hours to escape to a new location from which to horrify more humans.

The whole of the reptile section became my territory, as I learned some nifty tricks that helped me to escape at least twice a week. I must've broken some records with the number of humans I've caused to cry, fall over, wet themselves, or drop food; several humans have even left their young in front of me in their rush to escape my non-existent wrath (*luckily for their young I eat rodents, not humans*).

Eventually, the toll of my addiction has meant I've had to take life a little slower in my senior years. There are only so many times one can be trampled, slapped, squashed, and kicked before bodily functions are damaged. So, scare humans if you like, but know that it comes at a price, and you *will* lose cloaca control.

Contributor #15
Penguin

Love is powerful. No-one knows where it comes from or how it is formed, but everyone knows how incredibly awesome love's impact is on the joyfulness of life.

As a species, we are monogamous for life, and it is a proud trait we share with humanity. I have noted the human capacity for love, and it's wonderful to watch love blossom between two humans. My mate and I actually met during a human observation session! So, we regularly take a step back from the hustle of daily life to watch humans fall in love from the very spot we fell for each other a decade ago. It's ever so romantic.

But we have noticed that a few evil humans believe it acceptable to select several mates without revealing to any of them that they are *sharing* the original human's affections. I know my mate was as shocked as me to discover that humans were capable of such dreadful deceit, and together we decided to do something about it.

The human in question was a regular visitor to our habitat, so we could recognise him from quite a distance. My mate and I would search the crowds for the unfaithful human and make a mental note of his appearance. We remembered the annual 'meet the humans' event was fast approaching, and that the traitorous human had attended every year since he was young. While my mate and I were disappointed not to be revelling in the company of nice humans, we felt it more important to punish the adulterous human for his terrible behaviour. Also, during the build-up to that day, we had informed the flock of our plan and they kindly agreed to support us.

So, the special event arrived, and, sure enough, the cheater was in attendance. As the humans piled into our habitat, excited at the prospect of interacting with the world's greatest divers, we concentrated on our mission. The fraudulent human was towards the end of a line, and fortunately, he was nearest the water's edge. While the keeper wowed the crowd with amazing facts about us, the entire flock poised ourselves for the 'fish toss' that followed the keeper's speech. As always, humans began flinging fish into the pool, and we all dived for them to a chorus of applause. Then, we timed our emergence from the water perfectly, as we piled out almost as one and dropped mushed up fish onto the cheating one's shiny feet. Crowds burst into laughter, chattering excitedly as they checked their devices were recording. We never saw the double-crossing human again. Hooray!

Note from the Author

Thank you for purchasing this book. I hope you enjoyed the 'contributions' within…

If you'd like to discover more of my writing, please do any – or all – of the following:

Visit my website:
https://www.dekendall.com/

'Like' my Facebook™ page:
@dekendallauthor

'Follow' my Instagram™ page:
@d.e.kendall

Find me on Twitter™:
@DEKendall1

Reviews are important because they help readers discover their next favourite read and/or author. If you've kindly crafted a review of my work, you are amazing, and I am beyond thankful.

Happy reading!

9 7 9 8 8 4 8 2 2 0 2 0 9